Using this book

When going through this book
with your child, you can either read through
the story first, talking about it
and discussing the pictures,
or start with the sounds pages
at the beginning.

If you start at the front of the book,
read the words and point to the pictures.
Emphasise the **sound** of the letter.

Encourage your child to think
of the other words beginning with
and including the same sound.
The story gives you the opportunity
to point out these sounds.

After the story, slowly go through the
sounds pages at the end.

Always praise and encourage
as you go along. Keep your
reading sessions short and stop
if your child loses interest.

D0354370

Throughout the series, the order in which the sounds
are introduced has been carefully planned to
help the important link between reading and writing.
This link has proved to be a powerful boost to
the development of both skills.

SOUNDS FEATURED IN THIS BOOK

e c o s er ew ee ea
'magic'e cr cl ch oo oa or
ou ow sn sp sh st sk

The sounds introduced are repeated
and given emphasis in the practice books,
where the link between reading and writing is at the
root of the activities and games.

A catalogue record for this book is available
from the British Library

Published by Ladybird Books Ltd
A subsidiary of the Penguin Group
A Pearson Company
© LADYBIRD BOOKS LTD MCMXCIII

LADYBIRD and the device of a Ladybird are trademarks of
Ladybird Books Ltd Loughborough Leicestershire UK

Text copyright © Jill Corby MCMXCIII

Say the Sounds
Rocket
to the jungle

by JILL CORBY

illustrated by MIMI EVERETT

Ee

Say the sound.

elephant

egg

red

Cc

Say the sound.

castle

candle

cat

Oo

octopus

clock

dog

on

top

not

hot

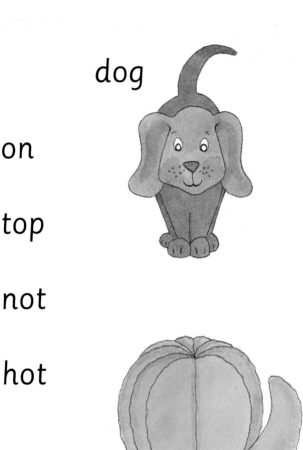

orange

Ss

sun

sea

sand

8

end **S**

socks

sails

sees   says   sits

Jenny

Ben

Ben and Jenny

Here is Ben

and here is Jenny.

Ben is here
and Jenny is here.

Ben has a crocodile.
Jenny has an elephant.

Jenny is on the elephant.

Ben is on the crocodile.

An octopus sees Ben.

A snake sees Jenny.

Jenny has the octopus
on the elephant.

Ben has the snake on
the crocodile.

22

Where is the elephant?
Where is the snake?

An octopus was in here.

Is it an octopus? No!

An elephant was
in here.

Is it an elephant? No!

The crocodile was
in here.

Is it a crocodile? No!

The snake was in here.

Is it a snake? No!

Where is the elephant now?

And where is the snake?

Jenny sees the crocodile.

Ben sees the octopus.

Where is Ben now?
Where is Jenny now?

Goodbye! Goodbye!
Goodbye!

er

over

river

under

diver

ew

new

few

dew

screw

ee

bee

tree

see

feet

cheese

green

ea

seat

eat

meat

seal

ea

head

dead

feather

34

'magic' **e** makes the sound <u>underlined</u> – say its name.

c<u>a</u>ke   l<u>i</u>ke

b<u>i</u>ke

h<u>o</u>me

teleph<u>o</u>ne

h<u>u</u>ge

c<u>u</u>be

cr

crown

crayons

cry

crash

cl

clown

climb

cloud

ch

chocolate

children

chick

chain

ch

sandwich

rich

torch

arch

Say the sounds.

oo

moon

food

balloon

zoo

oo This **oo** sound is different.

good

look

book

wood

oa

boat

coat

road

soap

or

horse

fork

horn

port

ou

mouse

mountain

ow

flower

brown

ow

arrow

This **ow** sound is different.

yellow

sn

snake

sneeze

snow

sp

spin

spider

speak

sh

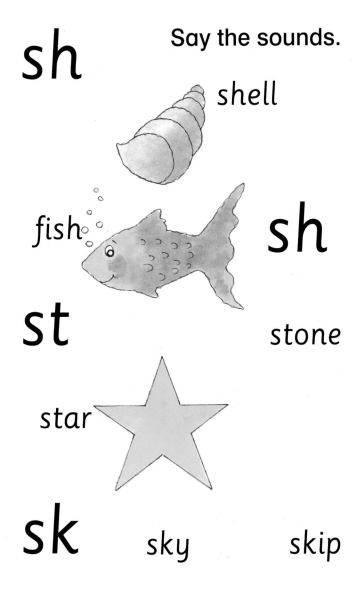

shell

fish

sh

st

stone

star

sk

sky

skip

42

New words used in the story

Words introduced   22

Learn to read with Ladybird

Read with me

A scheme of 16 graded books which uses a look-say approach to introduce beginner readers to the first 300 most frequently used words in the English language (Key Words). Children learn whole words and, with practice and repetition, build up a reading vocabulary.

Support material: Pre-reader, Practice and Play Books, Book and Cassette Packs, Picture Dictionary, Picture Word Cards

Say the Sounds

A phonically based, graded reading scheme of 8 titles. It teaches children the sounds of individual letters and letter combinations, enabling them to feel confident in approaching Key Words.

Support material:
Practice Books, Double Cassette Pack, Flash Cards

Read it yourself

A graded series of 24 books to help children to learn new words in the context of a familiar story. These readers follow on from the pre-reading series, **Read together**, and can be used in conjunction with any Ladybird reading scheme.